With love and
thanks to Nat
—Giles

For Justin,
the best daddy
in the world
—Emma x

Text copyright © 2011 by Giles Andreae
Illustrations copyright © 2011 by Emma Dodd
First published in Great Britain in 2011 by Orchard Books,
an imprint of Hachette Children's Books.

First U.S. edition, 2012
10 9 8 7 6 5 4 3 2 1
R969-8180-0-12001
Printed in China

Library of Congress Cataloging-in-Publication Data

Andreae, Giles, 1966–
   I love my daddy / Giles Andreae & [illustrated by] Emma Dodd.
      p. cm.
   Summary: A father and child enjoy special time together
playing on the swings, singing and dancing, having snacks, and
cuddling.
   ISBN 978-1-4231-4328-4 (hardcover)
   [1. Stories in rhyme. 2. Father and child—Fiction.] I. Dodd,
Emma, 1969– ill. II. Title.
   PZ8.3.A54865Iam 2012
   [E]—dc22   2011011094

Reinforced binding

Visit www.disneyhyperionbooks.com

I love my daddy

Giles Andreae
& Emma Dodd

 · HYPERION BOOKS
NEW YORK

I love my daddy, yes I do,

He's very kind—and funny too.

He teaches lots of things to me,

I think he's clever. So does he!

He lets me climb up on his back,

And we play horsies—*click clack clack*.

He sings me all his favorite songs,

I love to dance and sing along.

His shoes are very big and brown,

They make me look just like a clown!

He lifts me on his shoulders high,

Until I nearly touch the sky.

And when we're playing on the swings,

He does all sorts of silly things.

For fun, when Mommy's not at home,

We sometimes watch TV alone!

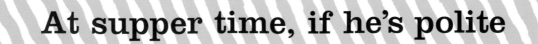

At supper time, if he's polite

I always let him have one bite.

I really love to cuddle him,

And feel the prickles on his chin.

He tucks me safely into bed,

Then tells me stories from his head.

My daddy's such a lovely man,

In fact, I am his BIGGEST fan!